GOLDILOCKS AND THE THREE BEARS

Retold by Jim Aylesworth

Illustrated by Barbara McClintock

Scholastic Press • New York

An early version of this beloved story was entitled "The Story of the Three Bears" and was written down in 1837 by a poet named Robert Southey. Today, he is most remembered with Coleridge and Wordsworth as one of the Lake Poets. Southey's version featured an old woman instead of a little girl. As storytellers told and retold his story, the old woman disappeared in favor of the little girl. Her name, of course, is Goldilocks, and she is one of the best-recognized characters in children's books. Special thanks to Karen Van Rossem for her help in tracing the history of this story. Excellent source notes can be found in *The Classic Fairy Tales* by Iona and Peter Opie, Oxford University Press, 1974.

Library of Congress Cataloging-in-Publication Data
Aylesworth, Jim.
Goldilocks and the three bears / retold by Jim Aylesworth;
illustrated by Barbara McClintock.   p. cm.
Summary: A little girl walking in the woods finds the house of the three
bears and helps herself to their belongings.
ISBN 0-439-39545-3
[1. Folklore. 2. Bears—Folklore.] I. McClintock, Barbara, ill. II.
Goldilocks and the three bears English. III. Title.
PZ8.A95 Go 2003   398.22–dc21   2002015964

Book design by David Saylor
The text type was set in 14-point Edwardian Medium.
The display type was hand lettered by Kevin Pyle
The artwork was rendered in watercolor, sepia ink, and gouache.

10 9 8 7 6 5 4   04 05 06 07
Printed in Singapore 46   First edition, September 2003

To Robert Southey, with admiration and thanks!
— J. A.

To David A. Johnson and Lainie Noonan, with love
— B. M.

Once upon a time, there lived a little girl named Goldilocks, who was very, very good, except that sometimes she forgot to do things that her mother told her to do. Yes she did.

Fortunately, most of the things she forgot to do were small things, like forgetting to tie her shoe or forgetting to wipe her mouth after eating bread and jam, and so it didn't matter too, too much.

But once in a while, Goldilocks would forget not to do things that her mother told her not to do, and that kind of forgetting would lead to much more serious trouble. . . .

. . .Very like the trouble that happened on the day of this story.

It all began one sunny morning when Goldilocks asked if she could go out onto the meadow to pick flowers.

"You may go," said her mother. "But make sure not to go into the woods! I've heard that a family of bears lives there."

"Yes, ma'am!" said Goldilocks, and she picked up her flower basket and she left out the door.

But very soon, she saw a butterfly, and she began to chase it. And, as luck would have it, that butterfly led her to the very edge of the woods. And then, just then, Goldilocks saw a pretty yellow bird. And wanting to see more pretty birds, she forgot not to do what her mother told her not to do, and she followed a path up into the woods looking for pretty birds.

Very soon, Goldilocks came to a curious
little house there in the woods.

And oh, she thought it was so pretty that
straight away she peeked in through the
kitchen door.

In the meantime, the family of bears who lived there had just left out the front door for a walk while their bowls of breakfast porridge cooled off on their kitchen table.

"Hello!" called Goldilocks. "Anybody home?"

Well, there was nobody home, of course, and Goldilocks should have turned around and gone back to the meadow.

But oh, it was ever so pretty and curious inside there, that, even though her mother had told her not to go into people's houses without being invited, she forgot not to, and she went in anyway.

Straight away, she saw those porridge bowls on the kitchen table. And *mmm*, yes! That porridge smelled so delicious that I'm afraid she forgot that her mother had told her not to touch other people's food, and she decided that she had to have a taste. And she did.

First, she took a taste from the great, huge papa-bear bowl, but oh my, no! That porridge was much too hot!

So then, she took a taste from the middle-sized mama-bear bowl, but that porridge was too cold.

And so then, she took a taste from the wee, small baby-bear bowl, and she found it neither too hot nor too cold, but just right. And so delicious, that without really meaning to, she ate it all up.

Then, she went into the parlor. And there, she saw three curious chairs. Goldilocks thought they were the most curious chairs that she had ever seen.

In fact, they seemed so curious to her that even though her mother had told her not to use people's things without permission, she forgot not to, and she climbed up, and she sat down in the great, huge papa-bear chair.

But after only a moment or two, she found that this great, huge chair was much too hard for her.

So she climbed down, and she sat in the medium-sized mama-bear chair. But this chair was too soft for her.

So next, she sat in the wee, small baby-bear chair. And this chair she found neither too hard nor too soft, but just right.

But when she leaned back to make herself more comfortable, it broke and dropped her onto the floor with a *CRASH!*

Well, you might think that being dropped on the floor like that would have put a stop to her being so curious, but no, it didn't, sadly no.

For just then, Goldilocks saw the curious little stairs, and she was so intrigued that she went up them.

At the top, she found an even more curious and pretty room, and even though her mother had often told her not to be nosy about other people's private business, she forgot not to, and she went in. And there she saw three curious beds.

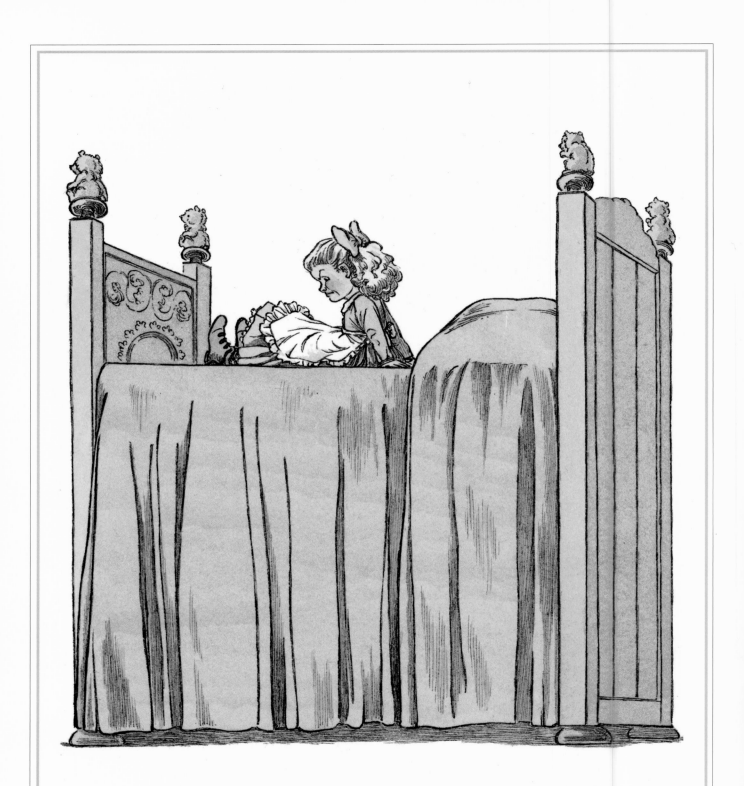

And straight away, she climbed up into the great, huge papa-bear bed.
But very like the great, huge papa-bear chair, Goldilocks found it too
hard for her.

So she tried the medium-sized mama-bear bed, but like the mama-bear chair, she found it too soft for her.

And so last, she tried the wee, small baby-bear bed. And yes, she found it neither too hard nor too soft, but just right. And so very, very comfortable that without really meaning to, she fell sound asleep.

Then, just then, the bear family returned from their walk.

The great, huge papa bear went over to the kitchen table, and in his great, huge voice, he said,

"Someone's been eating my porridge!"

Then the mama bear looked at her bowl, and in her
medium-sized voice, she said,
   "Someone's been eating my porridge!"

And then the baby bear
looked at his bowl, and in his
wee, small voice, he said,
   "Someone's been eating my
porridge, and they ate it all up!"

Then they went into the parlor.

"Someone's been sitting in my chair!"

said the papa bear in his great, huge voice.

"And someone's been sitting in my chair!"
said the mama bear in her medium-sized voice.

"And someone's been sitting in my chair!"
cried the baby bear in his wee, small voice.
"And they broke it all up!"

Cautiously, the bears went up the stairs.

The papa bear looked at his bed, and in his great, huge voice, he said,

"Someone's been sleeping in my bed!"

"And someone's been sleeping in my bed!"
said the mama bear in her medium-sized voice.

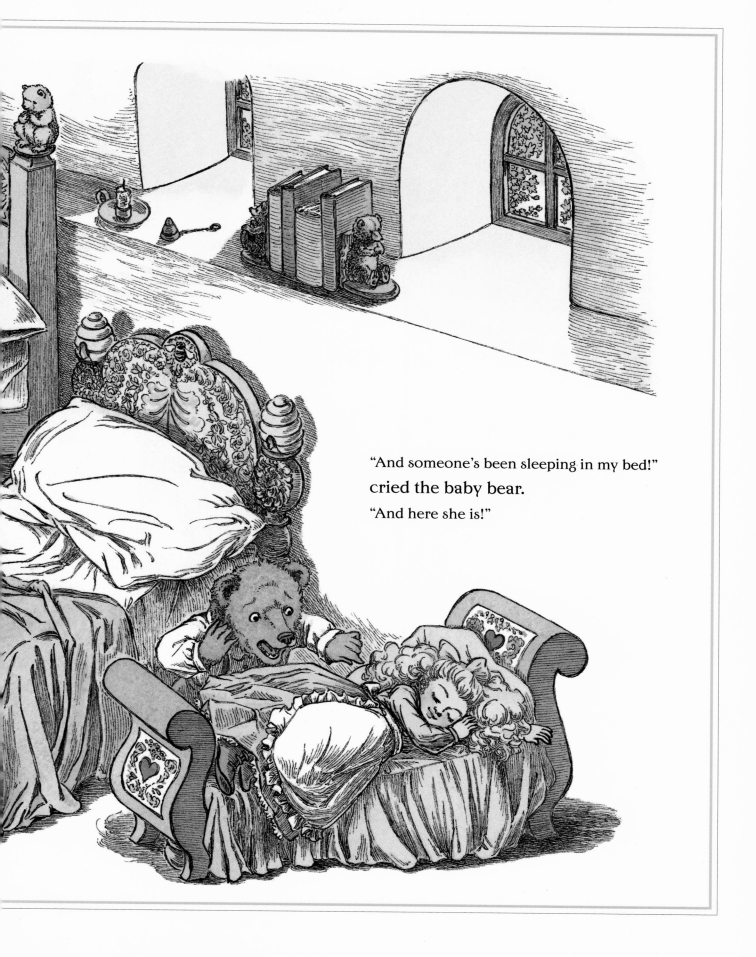

"And someone's been sleeping in my bed!"
cried the baby bear.
"And here she is!"

Then, just then, Goldilocks woke up, and she looked up at the bears who were looking at her! And just as fast, she remembered that her mother had told her not to talk to strangers, and she didn't do it! No, indeed, she didn't!

Instead, she ran down the stairs,

and she ran through the kitchen and she ran out the door. . .

. . . and she ran, and she ran, and she ran all the way home.

And from all that I've heard, Goldilocks's scary experience there in the woods that day did wonders to improve her young memory. And while it's true that she still sometimes forgets to do small things like tying her shoe or wiping her mouth after eating bread and jam, Goldilocks never, ever forgot not to do what her mother told her not to do ever, ever, ever again.